THE KINGDOM REVEALED

Rob Ryan

Crocodile Books, USA

An imprint of Interlink Publishing Group, Inc.

www.interlinkbooks.com

I T'S BEEN A SUNNY DAY and I've spent most of it here in the park, enjoying the warm weather, but now it's beginning to get dark and quite cold. I think I'll leave soon and head back home.

But what if I didn't have a home to go back to? What would I do then? Perhaps I could stay with my family or a friend. But what if I didn't have any family or friends, no one to turn to at all? What if I were completely and utterly alone in this big city, with nothing except the clothes on my back? No money in my pocket and no means of getting any. What on earth would I do?

Sadly, this story is all about someone who found themself in exactly that position. It's about a boy who ran away from home and left everything he had ever known behind.

BUT THERE WAS SOMETHING DIFFERENT about this particular runaway, which you may find hard to believe. Not only was he penniless, homeless, and friendless; he was also the King.

A little while ago, before his father died and he took his place as ruler of the Kingdom, this boy had discovered a hidden door in the ceiling above his grand four-poster bed.

While the palace was sleeping he had walked a long-forgotten passageway, containing a small window that had been painted over. For the first time in years, he had opened it. Night after night he had snuck out and explored the city all on his own, always returning before dawn. He had never told anyone his secret.

ONE MORNING, the young King didn't come back.

It was none other than the most senior of all the King's courtiers, Lord Von Dronus, who discovered that the Royal bedchamber was empty. "This is bad, this is very bad," he muttered to himself. "This must be concealed; this must be contained."

Leaving the room, Von Dronus locked the door behind him. Addressing the guards standing to attention outside, he said, "The King is ill and I fear he may be highly contagious. No one is to set foot inside the Royal bedchamber except myself. Understood?"

Lord Von Dronus stormed to his office. Since the King had been a small child, it had been Von Dronus's duty—one he took extremely seriously— to prepare the boy for the day when he would inherit his father's crown. He had long suspected that his charge had somehow found a way of getting out of the palace undetected—which in itself was most improper behavior—but the boy had always been where he should be in the morning.

The Lord's anger grew as he contemplated the implications of a monarch who had vanished. There was only one way to interpret the young King's disappearance: as a complete and utter betrayal which could not, nor would not, be tolerated.

As he stood looking out of his window at the vast city, Lord Von Dronus knew what he had to do. He would hunt the young King down and return him to the palace before anyone knew he'd gone.

THE KING was in the park. He had been wandering its criss-crossing paths for most of the morning.

The same things that you or I see every day, and think of as ordinary, seemed unusual and fascinating to his eyes. You have to remember that all of his life he had lived within the walls of a palace, and when, on rare occasions, he had left to attend an official function, he had always been the center of attention. Everything he'd ever seen, every smile and wave he'd ever made, had been carefully orchestrated.

No one he had ever met had acted naturally in front of him. Everyone was always on their best behavior.

Walking around the park he saw an old woman sitting on a park bench, feeding a few crumbs to some sparrows, and a man casually reading a newspaper. The King had never witnessed people jogging and exercising before; and he was completely spellbound.

He looked up and in the highest leaves of the trees he saw many brightly colored birds. *How exotic they look! How little I really know about my own country! I never knew we had such beautiful birds. It feels like I'm watching a film, except I'm actually inside it, walking around. It's as if I'm invisible*, he thought to himself.

It was a magical morning, full of wonder, and the young King felt like he didn't have a care in the world.

H E LEFT THE PARK and walked until he came upon a busy train station.

There were crowds of people everywhere he looked. Loudspeakers boomed
out the times of arrivals and departures, engines rumbled and roared as trains
pulled in and out of their platforms, and the sound of a thousand footsteps and voices
echoed in the cavernous hall.

It all seemed totally terrifying and exciting at the same time, something more full of life

Who are all these people? Where are they going? the young King wondered as he watched the crowds stroll and stride, and even run, in every possible direction, weaving in and around each other but never once colliding.

It's like the ballet: it looks confusing at first, but everybody knows their part, everyone seems to have somewhere they need to be going.

And he stood on the parapet and watched the amazing scene beneath him.

THE REST OF THAT day he wandered the streets with neither purpose nor direction. Time and again he noticed things that struck him as incredible. He saw that some people wore clothes of black or brown or gray, as if they wanted to blend in with the brick and concrete on the street and disappear, while others wore bright colors and vibrant shapes, as if to say, *Look at me! See how fabulous I look!*

He realized that the people in his very own city were from every corner of the world, in every shade that human beings could be, all jumbled up and living together as if the whole world were in this one great place! And the variety of people walking on the street seemed almost infinite: fat and skinny, hairy and bald, tall and short. Every single type of person you could ever imagine seemed to pass him by on an endless conveyor belt.

As the day wore on he noticed the life of the city changing. At one point in the afternoon, schoolchildren seemed to be everywhere, pushing and shoving each other. But then, almost as quickly as they had appeared, they were gone, replaced by throngs of people escaping from their day's work, filling the sidewalks on their way to shops and cafés before heading home.

Just as the streets seemed to get quieter, a new crowd appeared, younger and jollier, and intent on seeking fun. Bright neon lights came on, advertising films and shows, and as he walked past bars and restaurants, roars of laughter and singing burst forth onto the street when their doors opened and closed.

It was only when the smell of food hit him that the young King realized how hungry he was.

"I haven't eaten anything all day," he said to himself. He had been so absorbed in everything he'd seen that he hadn't once thought about food.

But very soon the city changed once more as people filled the streets again, noisy and shouting and full of boisterous life. Men and women called out goodnight to each other as they got into taxis and onto buses, couples kissed in doorways, and merry folk weaved along the street, singing out of tune.

After a little while, the streets were quiet again and only he remained.

It was a lot for the city's latest visitor to take in, and as it was beginning to get cold, he decided to head back to the busy train station. At least there it would be warm.

IT WAS MUCH LATER than he had thought, and the last train had just left. The station's frantic energy had drained away as the day had ended, and now its huge hall was empty and quiet.

In the strange stillness an announcement crackled from the loudspeakers, seeming ten times louder than it really was. The single lonely voice bounced and echoed off the huge arched roof:

"THE STATION IS CLOSING IN FIVE MINUTES. PLEASE MAKE YOUR WAY TO THE NEAREST EXIT."

The young King's heart sank as exhaustion washed over him. He left the empty terminal and returned to the place where his day had begun that morning, although

As HE WALKED down the street there was no one anywhere except a young couple walking on the same sidewalk, a short way ahead of him.

He could just make out the girl say to her friend, "I can't eat any more. I'm absolutely full."

"Your eyes are too big for your stomach," her friend replied, and as they passed a trash can the young King saw her toss something into it.

As he walked past the trash can he smelled a delicious salt and vinegar aroma and, peering in, he saw a half-eaten bag of fries. He reached in and pulled them out. They were still hot, and he ravenously devoured every one. In all the time he had lived in the palace he had only ever been served the very finest food by the greatest chefs, but these fries were the most delicious thing he had ever tasted.

In the park it was dark and shadowy, and as he walked along the paths he gathered as many pieces of newspaper from the trash as he could. Finding a snug space beneath a bush, he covered himself with them in an attempt to get warm.

He looked up to the sky and directly above him a small flock of birds flew over, silhouetted against the full moon.

Those lucky birds, he thought, *flying home to their warm nests. I hope their families are glad to see them return.* And as he imagined the smiling beaks welcoming them all home, he fell asleep.

That night he had a strange dream, unlike any he'd ever had before. It was as if his very being had split into two separate and distinct parts, his mind and his body, and he could feel them talking to each other.

His mind spoke to his body and told it, "I will protect you," and in reply his body spoke to his mind and said, "I will protect you."

THE YOUNG KING AWOKE just as the sun was rising the following morning. He'd had a restless night and was shocked to find he was not in his comfortable four-poster bed, but lying under a bush, covered in newspapers.

It was already warm and looked like it was going to be another hot day. When he suddenly caught sight of his reflection in the window of an ice cream truck, his disheveled appearance came as quite a shock. *Good heavens! I look like I've been dragged through a bush*, he thought, and then he realized that he more or less had been, and to the bemusement of the people around him he laughed out loud.

Around a fountain was a ring of benches, so he sat down, facing the morning sun. All around him were mothers playing with their young children, and older people just sitting still, enjoying the peacefulness of a pleasant summer's morning. As he listened to the tinkling water in the fountain mingling with the happy sounds of children playing, his eyes closed and soon he was fast asleep.

He woke with a start hours later. *How long have I been asleep?* he wondered, and as he looked around he realized that the people had left while he had slept, all except one large bearded man sitting directly opposite him on the other side of the fountain. *Am I imagining it or is he smiling at me?* the young King thought, but just then, his stomach interrupted his thoughts with a loud rumble.

I've got to start getting organized. I need a place to sleep. Somewhere better than here. And food! I have no money, so I need some, but how do I get any? I need work. I'll start looking for a job, but how? How on earth do people find jobs? How does anyone do anything? I've got to pull myself together. I've got to get to grips with this new world or I might as well admit defeat and go back to the palace right now.

The young King's mind was going around in circles like this for a long time as he tried to work out a way to improve his situation, until suddenly his thoughts were interrupted by the big shaggy-looking man who had been sitting opposite him.

"Excuse me, son, is anyone sitting here?"

THE YOUNG KING LOOKED nervously at him, not knowing quite what to say.

The old hairy man said, "Well, I'll take that as a yes then," and he winked at him and smiled. "Are you waiting to meet anyone?" he asked next.

Afraid of giving away who he really was, the young King muttered "Yes," but only a dry croak came out of his mouth. He realized he hadn't spoken at all since leaving the palace.

Taking a banana from his bag, the old man handed it to him. And the two of them sat there together, slowly eating, the ravenous King savoring every precious bite.

"Have you got anywhere to stay?" the stranger asked once they had both finished eating.

The King hesitated before answering with a lie: "Yes, I do. I'm fine."

The old man smiled at him, and the young King saw a warmth in his eyes.

"Listen, son, there's nothing to be ashamed of if you haven't. Most people who have places to stay don't sit on the same bench for five hours at a time, and seeing the way you wolfed down that banana I'd say you haven't eaten a thing all day. Everybody needs a bit of help now and again. Do you know what? I was just like you, a long time ago. What about your mum—does she know you're okay?"

This last question caught the boy completely by surprise. He mumbled "No," and felt his eyes beginning to fill with tears.

"Well, just because you're unhappy it doesn't mean you have to make other people unhappy too." Suddenly the big old man got to his feet and began to gather his bags together.

"Listen, I'm going off to get something to eat. If you're still as hungry as you look, then you're welcome to come along with me—my name is Big Jim. If you don't want to, then that's fine too—suit yourself."

The young King smiled and got up too. "Thank you, thank you very much."

"Well, you have lovely manners. I see you haven't been raised by wolves. That'll take you a long way in life, son, mark my words."

The two of them headed off together, and it wasn't long before they arrived at a street that ran beneath the arches behind the train station. Here they came to a small van where a table had been set up, and from the van a large pot of lovely hot stew was being dished out to a line of about twenty people.

After they had eaten, the young King's new friend left for a while but soon returned with a big sweater and a thick sleeping bag. "It's summer now, but I can still show you a warmer place to sleep than the park," he said, and led him down a maze of side streets to a quiet alley you'd never even know was there. "Heat comes up from that vent. It'll keep you warm all night, and they throw out cardboard over there—you can use it to sleep on." Into his hand he thrust a fistful of money. "Call your mum and tell her that you're all right."

Before the young King could even thank him, the old man had already turned and headed off into the night.

WHEN THE KING WOKE up the next day he realized there was something he had to do.

He spent the morning looking for a safe place where he could hide his sleeping bag, and in the afternoon he made his way to a bus stop on a street just by the side of the palace. Eventually the person the King was looking for joined the line. This man was the only real friend he had ever had inside the palace, a lowly servant whose job it was to clean and polish everybody's boots and shoes, and the only person who always found time for him: the Bootman.

As the Bootman got on board, the young King furtively followed and sat a few seats behind him. After all the lonely hours he had spent on the street, it took every ounce of self-control not to go and talk to him.

When the Bootman finally got off the bus, the King followed him at a safe distance all the way back to his home. And not long after the Bootman had opened his front door and gone inside, the young King quickly ran up the path and pushed a note through the mail slot before scurrying away.

THE YOUNG KING SPENT hour after hour visiting every museum and art gallery in the city, and he went into every department store, public library, and church. Sometimes, as they were closing, he would hide away and sleep there all night.

One of his favorite places to sleep was the Science Museum, where he made his bed inside the boiler of an old steam train. Other nights he climbed into a tight space behind the organ pipes in the vast cathedral that rose high above all the other buildings. I think a lot of people would be scared to sleep by themselves in such quiet, dark places where they shouldn't really be, but not him. In a strange way he felt that because he had no place to call his own, he considered anywhere and everywhere in the city his home.

ONE EVENING, AS HE walked through the busy crowds, he saw a door open and a stream of people flow into the street. After the last person had trailed out he quickly slipped into the exit, and at the end of a dark corridor he walked through a doorway into a vast auditorium.

He quickly ducked beneath a huge velvet curtain and found himself in a narrow space behind the screen. Presently he heard voices as the audience for the next performance arrived, and suddenly there was an explosion of sound, light, and color as giant images appeared on the screen above him.

Of all of his hidden sleeping places in the city, this became his favorite, not so much because he got to watch films in the warmth, but because as he listened to the audiences laugh and gasp and weep and cheer, he felt closer to the hearts of his subjects than he ever had before. The memory of their joy kept him warm long after the last show had finished, and when he settled down to sleep, the sound of scurrying mice kept him company as they feasted on the remnants of popcorn that had fallen on the floor.

BACK IN THE ROYAL PALACE, as the Queen Mother was taking off her shoes after a long day, a tiny piece of paper fell out. The Bootman had found a way of delivering the young King's note to his mother.

Dear Mother, she read, *don't worry about me, I am fine, I am looking after myself, and one day when all is well we will meet again. I love you. Your son.*

As the Queen Mother folded up the piece of paper, she laughed to herself. *How did I ever produce such a melodramatic child!* she fondly thought. *He gets a bad dose of the flu and he thinks he'll never see me again. He must have got a servant to secretly smuggle it out of his bedroom to me, but all the same, what a sweet boy.*

THE YOUNG KING HAD settled into a routine of wandering the city, eating at the food van, and finding safe places to sleep at night. His spirits were high and hopeful as he slowly discovered his new life.

But after weeks of sunshine, there was a great downpour that continued relentlessly for days. Trying to stay out of the rain, he felt conspicuous as he loitered, killing time in order to keep dry. He felt like a shopper who never bought anything, a man who went to church but never prayed. He began to believe that his solitariness was completely apparent to everybody he saw.

Soon he didn't want to see other people, or for them to see him. He made his way to the cemetery on the outskirts of the city, sat on a gravestone and thought.

My clothes are dirty and I feel grubby both inside and out. The nothingness of this wandering life is sucking the soul out of me.

How do you build a new life out of nothing? All I'm doing is just surviving. I don't know anybody and I don't know what else to do.

And as he sat there, the dark cloud that had settled in his head seemed to get bigger and bigger. The only thing he could think of was to get up and keep walking. At least then it wasn't quite so cold.

Eventually, his feet led him to his old home, the palace. Inside the windows he saw warm lights and he imagined a hot, steaming bath with clean, dry clothes laid out, waiting for him, and he thought of how he could order anything he desired to eat or drink.

Small and bedraggled, the King spoke to the palace. "I thought that I was bigger than you. I really thought I could live without you and stand alone on my own two feet, but I was wrong."

As a crowd of people brushed past him, little hot tears fell from his eyes. *I've tried so hard to be true to myself, and look where it has got me. I thought I could just be like everybody else, but I was wrong. I have one person to say goodbye to, then tomorrow I'll return and surrender myself to you. You've won; you can have what's left of my life, forever.*

That EVENING THE YOUNG King returned to the food van for the last time.

"Come and sit with me, son," Big Jim called out to him. "You look like you've got the world's troubles on your shoulders. At least come and share them with me."

The young King explained how he had really come to say goodbye; he was leaving the city to go back to his mum.

"Do you know, lad, I never pry into people's personal lives, that's their business. But the way you talk it sounds as if what's waiting for you there is no good, no good at all, and however bad it seems here, it might be better to stay and stick it out, see what turns up—you never know!"

"But nothing ever turns up. I feel like I'm going round and round in circles, never getting anywhere. I feel I'll still be walking these cold, hard streets when I'm an old man!" And as soon as he realized what he had said, he blurted out, "I'm sorry, I didn't mean to offend you. I didn't mean—"

The old man cut him off. "No offense taken, none at all. And he took the young King's hand in his. "I think it is time for you to become a man."

The young King looked at him, perplexed. "But how? But when? What can I do?" he stammered.

"Listen, when I was only thirteen both my parents died and I was left alone to look after my younger brother and sister. I had to do it because it needed to be done, and that is when I became a man. You grow up and become a man when you begin to put other people before yourself."

The buses going across the bridge rumbled overhead as the two men sat facing each other.

"But what can I do to put anyone before myself? You're the only person I know!" the young King mumbled. "What have I got to offer? I'm penniless, I've got nothing. I'm the person who should be receiving help—me!"

THE HAIRY OLD MAN slowly shook his head. "That's where you've got it all wrong," he said, then looked deeply into the boy's eyes. "You think you don't have anything, but you do. You have a brain and you still have hope, and with these two things you can form a plan—at first only the smallest little plan, I admit, but you have to begin somewhere. All you have to do is make a start."

Raising his voice in exasperation, the boy exclaimed, "I'm so confused! What on earth can I do to start—start what?!"

The kind old man didn't get angry at this childish outburst; he just rested his hand gently on the young King's arm and spoke to him. "Well, for starters, why don't you go over to that girl there, slaving away on her own, and ask her if she needs any help? Why not start there?"

The young King looked across and saw someone pouring stew into the bowls of the waiting women and men, and he realized what Big Jim meant. He got up, walked over to her and said nervously, "Excuse me, do you need any help?"

She smiled and said, "Yes, please!" She asked him to go and pick up the empty bowls, which he did, and then she asked him to grab a broom and sweep around and he did that too; all evening he did this and he did that, trying to help in each and every way he could. At the end of the evening he approached the young woman, saying, "I could help tomorrow too if you'd like."

"Thank you," she replied with a warm, tired smile. "We always need help," and as she climbed into her van she asked him his name. The young King paused and then said, "John. My name is John."

And from that day to this he still doesn't know why he said that name; it just came out of his mouth from nowhere; it just felt right at the time, and he was known as John for the rest of his life.

"Hi, John. I'm June."

The next day, instead of returning to the palace as he'd planned, he went back to the food van and helped out. After the last people had been fed, June approached him.

"John, Dave and I could do with some help tomorrow morning, getting everything ready for the—"

"YES!" he said, almost a little too loudly, before she had even finished her sentence.

"Gosh! Well, I'm glad you're keen!" She laughed. "Do you know Green Street?" When he nodded eagerly, she said, "We'll pick you up on the corner at nine o'clock."

And that is how the King became John, a man.

THE NEXT DAY his new life began.

The rain that seemed like it would never end finally stopped, and the sun returned. The young King—or John, as I should remember to call him from now on—had never felt as happy as he did now, driving around the city in the old van. Though he never had to work in his life before, he soon discovered that he enjoyed it.

June told him how she had started the food van. Like him, when she had moved to the city, she didn't know anybody at all. She worked as a van driver, and as she drove around

the city she saw lots of people on the streets every day with no homes to go to. So one day she bought a big pot, and that evening she cooked a large stew and carried it down to a corner near her house where she always saw a lot of homeless people, and she fed them. Soon people heard about what she was doing, and more people turned up every day.

"One day the owner of a café on the same street came down to see me," she reminisced. "He was very angry and started shouting at me because he thought I was taking customers away from his café by giving out free food. But when he saw how poor they were he went away and the next evening he came back with an enormous bowl of goulash. And you know what he said? 'You made me ashamed to be a human being!' He really was a very sweet man, and he came back every night from then on with food to give me, and even started to get all his friends who owned restaurants and cafés to help me too—they all know each other in that business. And it just got bigger and bigger, until finally, I quit my job to do this all day. This is my job now: people give me food and I serve it out.

"People are so funny. They really want to help, but at first they feel too shy and awkward. Once you speak to them though, and just say you can do this or you can do that, they are always happy to help and they always say the same thing: 'Why didn't you ask sooner?!'"

And she burst out laughing.

EACH DAY SEEMED SWEETER than the one before, and although he was still sleeping outside, the sunny days and warm nights of summer went on and on. At first, as they drove around in the van, John was happy just to sit and listen as June and Dave chatted away. But when he got to know them better he spoke more often, and when he made his first joke, Dave said, "He's slowly coming out of his shell!" and they all laughed together.

The city looked like a different place viewed through the windows of the van. Sandwiched tightly between June and Dave in the small cab, he didn't feel quite so alone any more; in fact, he began to feel as if he was becoming a part of the city, rather than just someone looking in from outside.

After he had been working with them for a few weeks, they turned up at one of the cafés that regularly gave them food. Angelo, the owner of the café, who was normally so cheerful, was standing on the street outside in his apron, looking very agitated.

"I'm so sorry, I have nothing for you today. My best worker has left me and I'm struggling in the kitchen on my own."

June told him not to worry and asked if she could help at all.

Angelo, although exasperated, laughed nevertheless. "Not unless you know someone who could drop everything and start now!" he said.

June looked at John. "We can spare you if you want to give it a try?" she said.

"If you're sure, yes, I could do it!" John replied.

Suddenly Angelo grabbed him and gave him a huge bear hug. "My savior!" he said. "Come, let me get you an apron—we've got work to do!" and he led John to the kitchen.

MEANWHILE, BACK IN THE PALACE, Lord Von Dronus had gathered the Prime Minister and the Head of the Military to a secret meeting. The Lord had realized that he couldn't pretend the King's illness was contagious for much longer. People in the palace, the Queen Mother included, were beginning to question the strangeness of the situation.

As the Lord explained the reality of the situation to the two powerful men present, they both nodded gravely. When he had finished speaking, the Prime Minister spoke: "Lord Von Dronus, you have done the right thing, but now you must let us help you. As you are aware, there are special plans in place for handling such situations and now it is time to implement them."

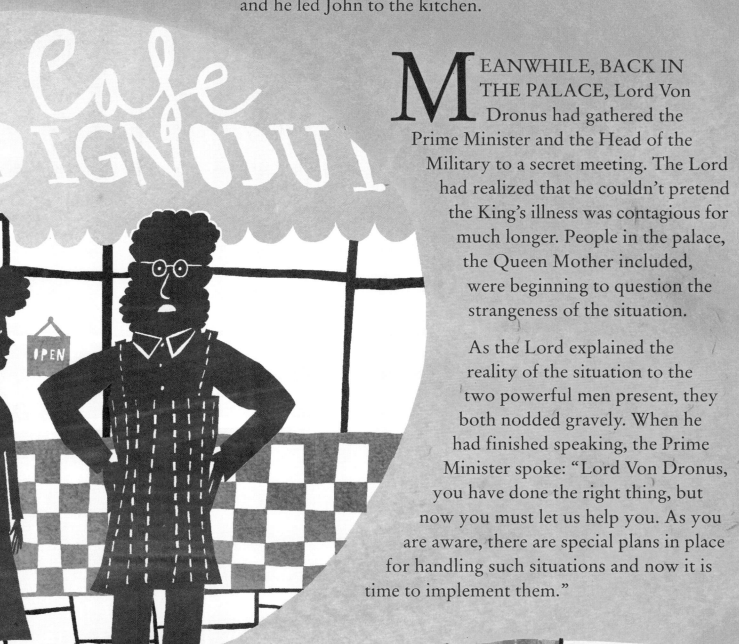

WITHOUT A PAUSE TO catch his breath, John set to work. The Café Dignodunrei was a hectic, busy place and everybody seemed to have twice as much work to do as they had time to do it in! Angelo's wife, Theresa, and his daughter, young Theresa, worked at the counter, taking orders and passing them to Angelo, who was the chef.

If a customer asked for two fried eggs on toast, Angelo would call out, "Driving Miss Googly Eyes!" Or if someone wanted a tuna roll he would shout, "Sea monster in his cave!" He had a funny phrase for everything on the menu and he was very proud of how he had made them up himself. After calling out, "Pebble-dashed submarines in a muddy sea!"—sausage and beans with brown sauce—

he turned to his new helper and proudly announced, "You know, Johnny boy, when I arrived in this beautiful country I couldn't speak a word of the language! Now look at me! I'm making up new sayings every day. What a world!"

As tiny and timid as his wife, Theresa, was, Angelo was big and noisy. That first morning it seemed to John that Angelo knew every customer by name, and even as he was bent over his chopping board with his back to them he would keep up his friendly chatter all day.

Finally, John's first day came to an end. Angelo asked the newcomer if he could work tomorrow too, then added, "Really, I would like you to take the job for good. I can see you are a hard worker, but much more importantly, I see you are a fine fellow."

That evening, exhausted from a hard day's work, John returned to see June at the food van. He felt embarrassed when he told her how Angelo had offered him a job, and added, "I don't know if I should take it."

A smile broke out on June's face. "That's brilliant news!" she said. "Of course you have to take it, you idiot."

"But I feel I'm letting you down."

"John, don't be crazy! Angelo and Theresa are good people, plus they can pay you, which we never could. This is a good chance for you, take it! Go back and say yes."

Deep inside, John knew she was right, but he couldn't help feeling sad. The days of driving around in the van had been so good, he wanted them to go on forever. Just then June, pretending to be angry with him, said, "But you'd better come back and visit us, because if you don't I'll chop you up and put you in a delicious stew and feed you to all these hungry fellows!" And then she, all the people in the line, and even John himself burst out laughing.

Life at the Café Dignodunrei was busy every day, but in the afternoon the staff stopped for a rest and in these quiet moments, Angelo and John got to know each other.

At the end of each working day, Angelo would make his wife Theresa sit down while he massaged her shoulders.

"Why would I want to go out and work for someone else when every day I have the pleasure of being with this most wonderful woman? Look at how lucky I am. What a world!"

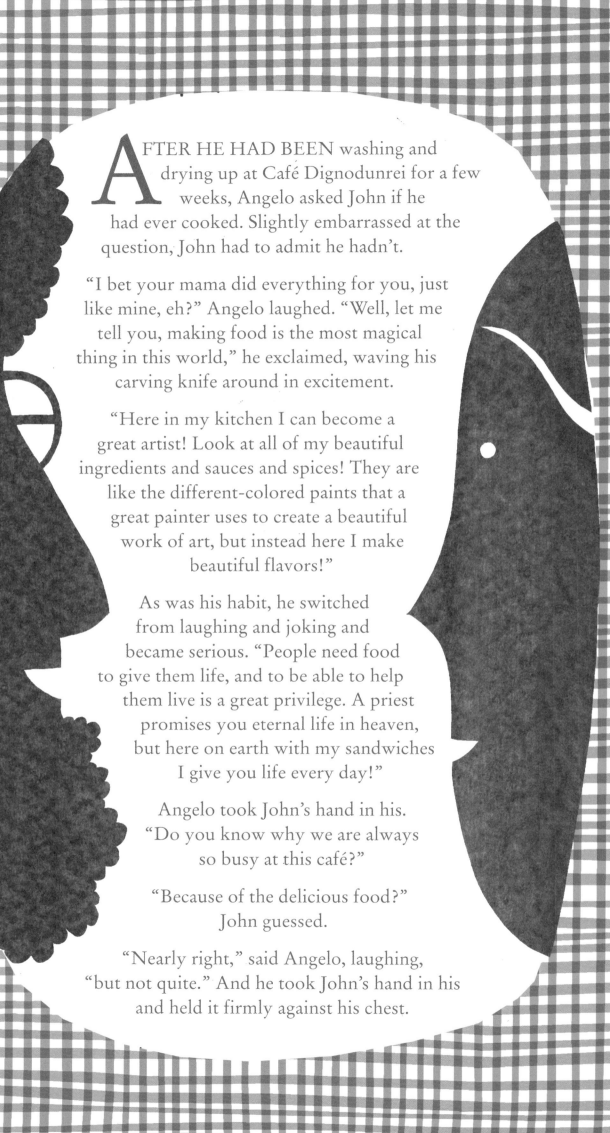

AFTER HE HAD BEEN washing and drying up at Café Dignodunrei for a few weeks, Angelo asked John if he had ever cooked. Slightly embarrassed at the question, John had to admit he hadn't.

"I bet your mama did everything for you, just like mine, eh?" Angelo laughed. "Well, let me tell you, making food is the most magical thing in this world," he exclaimed, waving his carving knife around in excitement.

"Here in my kitchen I can become a great artist! Look at all of my beautiful ingredients and sauces and spices! They are like the different-colored paints that a great painter uses to create a beautiful work of art, but instead here I make beautiful flavors!"

As was his habit, he switched from laughing and joking and became serious. "People need food to give them life, and to be able to help them live is a great privilege. A priest promises you eternal life in heaven, but here on earth with my sandwiches I give you life every day!"

Angelo took John's hand in his. "Do you know why we are always so busy at this café?"

"Because of the delicious food?" John guessed.

"Nearly right," said Angelo, laughing, "but not quite." And he took John's hand in his and held it firmly against his chest.

"The secret is because we make our food with love, from the heart, and we do our best for everybody. The poorest and the richest person all get the same treatment. Did you know that the digestive system of a king is exactly the same as that of the poorest servant?"

Angelo stretched out his arms as wide as he could as if to encompass the entire café and everything in it. He swelled up with pride as he exclaimed, "And that is why we are called Café Digno Dun Rei! It means 'The Café Fit for a King!'"

AS JOHN WAS STILL without somewhere to live, he was always the first to arrive at work and the last to leave.

"Let yourself in from now on," said Angelo as he pressed a key into John's hand. "And on Sunday, please come and have lunch with us at our home. I hate the thought of you being alone all day!" and he crushed John in yet another of his famous hugs.

Receiving the key to the café couldn't have been better timed. The summer was ending, and as the colder autumn nights approached, John would come back to the café late in the evening and sleep there in the warm.

Now he had a paying job the young King began to think about finding a place to live. In the window of a newsstand near the café, he noticed lots of advertisements for rooms to rent. Seeing a few he could afford, he began to work out the math to see how long he would need to save up for his deposit and first month's rent.

On Saturday afternoon, after he had been paid, for the first time in his life, John went shopping. He visited nearly every single shop in the city, looking at nothing but table forks. He held and tested every single fork until he found the one he liked the best, and then he bought it for himself.

Later that afternoon he heard a newspaper seller call out, "Young King at death's door! Read all about it!" An old lady standing beside John gasped out loud in shock. A small crowd was beginning to gather around an electrical shop window, listening in stunned silence to the newscaster describe how the King's illness had taken a sudden and serious turn for the worse.

It was a peculiar feeling for the young man to stand there, hearing episodes from his own life, as if it were nothing but a story that somebody else had written. He felt like a puppet, powerless to control his own existence.

THE FOLLOWING DAY was Sunday, and he made his way to Angelo and Theresa's crowded home for lunch.

"We've heard all about you, John!" all the children exclaimed excitedly, as they begged him to play with them.

"Angelo and Theresa think a lot of you, John. You must be a good fellow," said the older relatives, vigorously shaking his hand and kissing him on both cheeks.

"We have a special guest today. This young man who has come to us is all alone in this city, with no family, but he mustn't worry because we will be his new family here."

Everyone around the table nodded. Angelo added a special prayer for the recovery of the very ill young King, then everyone said "Amen" and began to eat.

Surprised yet intrigued by Angelo offering a prayer for the King, John asked him what he thought of the young monarch.

"To tell the truth, I don't know much about this young fellow, but if he turns out to be anything like his father then he will be a wonderful king! What a great man he was!"

John had never heard anybody praise his father like this. He had always assumed that this shy, reclusive man would not be thought of affectionately by his subjects. As a king he had hardly ever left his study, let alone appeared in public.

Angelo went on, "A few years ago I had some trouble and, not knowing who to turn to for help, I wrote in desperation to the King, asking his advice, and straight away he wrote back to me with very good advice and sensible words, like you would hear from your own papa."

And then Theresa added, "And do you remember he replied when I told him about my back?"

"And me too," piped up young Theresa, "when I was being bullied at school!"

One by one, each person sitting around the table had a similar story to tell (or knew somebody who had) about writing to the old King and of him writing back to them.

LATER THAT evening, after he had made his farewells to Angelo and his family, John walked through the park in the light of the full moon.

High up on a marble pedestal stood a statue of his father seated upon a horse. Standing beneath him his son shouted up into the cold night air, "Who were you? Somebody that I never knew. All the kindness you shared in all those countless letters! Why didn't you show any of it to me? Why didn't you let me in, instead of shutting yourself away?"

Tears welled up in his eyes as he stood there in the moonlight. He thought of all the warmth and love that flowed so easily between Angelo and Theresa, and how he couldn't remember ever seeing a loving glance pass between his parents.

"Am I doomed to end up like you? Locking my heart and love away from everyone, with only my secrets to keep me company? Only able to show love and kindness through ink flowing from a pen?"

And as he stood there that night he made a promise to himself: "I won't be like you."

As fast as he could, he went to where the food van was always parked. June was there, standing at her trestle table, ladling out hot food to a line of cold and hungry strangers.

He walked up behind her. "Hello," he said shyly.

She turned and gave him a wide grin. "Hello yourself! How lovely to see you."

And he stood there staring at this good, kind person long after she had turned back to resume her ladling. "It's so good to see you!" he finally blurted out, slightly too loudly, and then he hesitated a moment before adding, "I've missed you so much . . . and I think you are really . . . really . . ."

She turned around and laughed. "Well, what am I?! I haven't got all day, you know."

He stood there, staring at her dumbfounded, until finally a word jumped out of his mouth. "Brilliant," he said. "I think you are brilliant."

O NCE A week he would spend the whole afternoon walking from shop to shop, looking to buy one particular thing, just as he had done when he'd bought his fork.

One week it would be a plate, the next a mug, a spoon, a blanket, a knife, a sheet, or a glass.

When he had chosen and paid for the thing he wanted, he took it back to the café and hid it in the back of a cupboard. He put away the remaining money in a small box, and because he didn't have to spend any money on food, he managed to save almost all of his wages every week.

Every evening after work he would rush straight from the café to help out June and Dave at the food van. By the time they had finished at the end of the night he was utterly exhausted, and wherever he slept during those early autumn nights, be it by a heat vent in a dark doorway, or on the floor in the café, or even under a bench in the park, he fell immediately into a deep and heavy sleep.

But Sunday was the one day he had completely to himself. Usually he would fill the hours walking around the park and streets of the city, sometimes returning to the museums and galleries where he used to linger for hours in the long days after he had left the palace.

One day he took a bus out of the city and for hours he wandered alone through the fields and meadows. After a few hours he lay down in the long soft grass and took a rest.

Looking up,
he saw an airplane
high in the sky. It looked
about the size of a fly
and he remembered
how years ago, when
he was a small boy, he had
flown in an airplane for the first
time. He recalled how, as the plane
broke through the clouds, he
could suddenly see roads and
fields and houses, and they
all looked so very tiny. John
thought how, if he was up in that
plane right now, he would not even be
visible. He would seem so insignificant as
to almost not even exist, and as he
felt himself becoming ever
smaller and smaller he
felt happy and tired and his
eyes closed and he drifted off
in the afternoon sun.

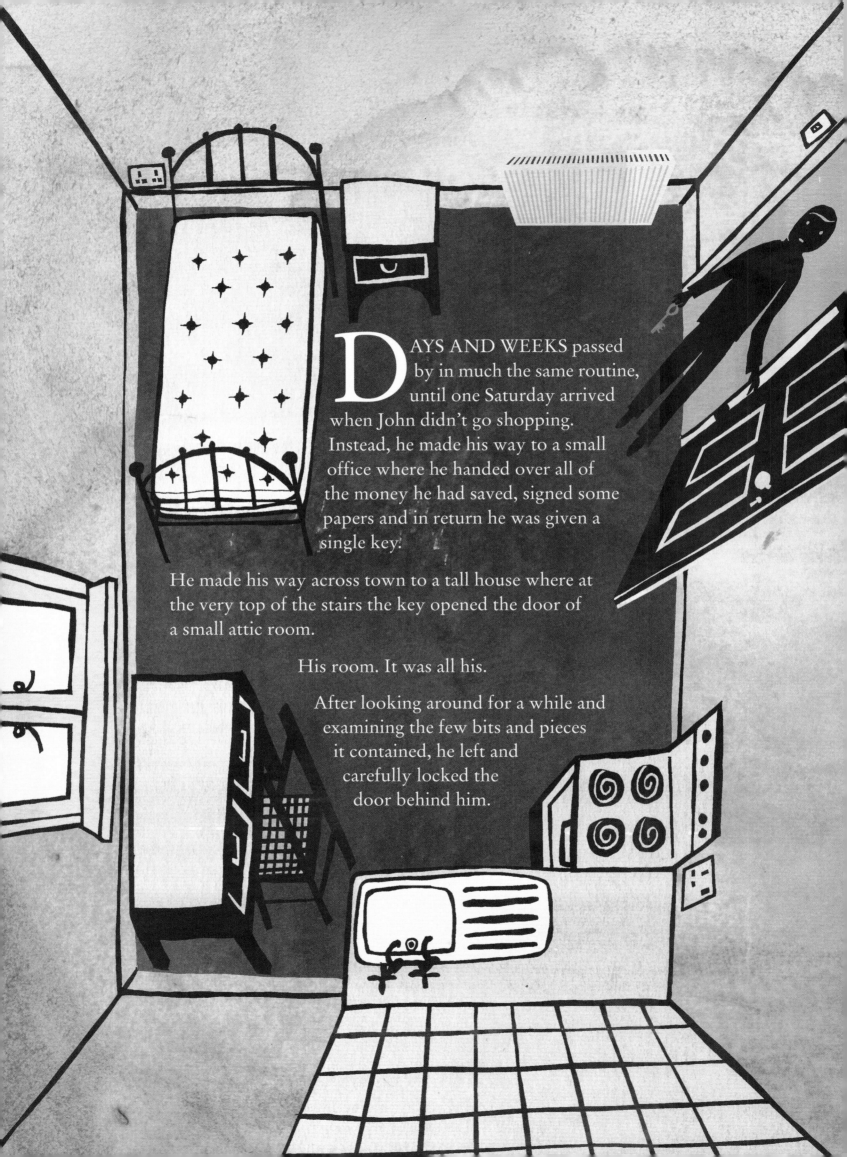

DAYS AND WEEKS passed by in much the same routine, until one Saturday arrived when John didn't go shopping. Instead, he made his way to a small office where he handed over all of the money he had saved, signed some papers and in return he was given a single key.

He made his way across town to a tall house where at the very top of the stairs the key opened the door of a small attic room.

His room. It was all his.

After looking around for a while and examining the few bits and pieces it contained, he left and carefully locked the door behind him.

Returning to the café, he picked up the small number of belongings he had been collecting ever since he had started his job.

When he returned to the room, he took out the sheets he had been saving for this day. He put them on the bed, followed by the blankets and the cover. Then he put the pillowcase on the pillow.

He didn't once sit or lie on the bed. He made himself a small and simple meal, then went for a walk around his new neighborhood.

It was a quiet area and a peaceful night.

When he returned to his new home he sat at his small table and read, and when he felt his eyes beginning to close he put his book down.

He went to the bathroom down the hall and ran a deep hot bath.

He washed his hair and scrubbed himself all over, then dried himself and got into the new pajamas that he had been warming on the radiator.

And then he finally did what he had been dreaming of for weeks and weeks: he pulled back the covers of his little bed and climbed in between the crisp white sheets. Warm and clean and smelling a little soapy, he closed his eyes and felt that this was the most wonderful thing in the world.

That night he dreamed the same strange dream he had had the very first night he had slept in the park. His mind and body talked to each other, but this time they spoke in unison, together as one.

"We made it, we survived, we made it, we survived."

H E ROSE ESPECIALLY early the next day and made his way to a Sunday street market where he bought an old bicycle and a bag of tools.

That afternoon he rode for hours and hours, deep into the countryside.

Pushing his pedals as hard as he could, he rode his bicycle to the top of a small hill where he unpacked his sandwiches in the shade of a tree. The pleasure of eating them after so much exertion was immense, and as he looked out across the hills and valleys he saw the great city in the distance and for some reason this thought came into his head:

I'm not going to look back any more. I'm only ever going to look forward.

NOW THAT AUTUMN had truly arrived the trees began to shed their leaves, and on his way home from work, John would pass by the park and spend a quiet hour collecting the ones he liked best.

On those windy evenings he would amuse himself for hours decorating his little room. Sorting the leaves into shapes and sizes, he then glued them onto the walls.

The nights got shorter and shorter, and after a quiet evening of decorating and reading he would sit by his window and listen to the wind whistle angrily outside as the rain pattered constantly against the glass.

What a miracle it is to be inside four strong walls with a roof above me, warm and snug, unlike so many out there on this cold night, he thought to himself.
How lucky I am.

THE NEXT EVENING, instead of going home to his warm room, he went to help out again at the food van.

"Now the winter is coming we will get busier and busier," June said as she washed up and John dried. "More and more mouths to feed every night."

"You must have made food for tens of thousands of people over the years," John said as they finished packing away the pots and bowls. "Just for a change, will you let me make a meal for you?"

The young man's face blushed red as June laughed and said, "Ha! I thought you'd never ask! OK, it's a date!"

As he sped down a hill on the way home, the evening air rushed past his face, and every single nerve in his body seemed alive and full of joy.

I never realized that life could feel as sweet as this, he thought.

EVERY EVENING THAT WEEK, as soon as he had left work, John would go shopping, zigzagging from store to store. He would carefully choose one more thing of everything he already possessed: one more fork, one more knife, one more spoon, plate, glass, napkin, and bowl, so that by Saturday he would be ready to host his guest.

Table Knives

NAPKINS

SPOONS

J OHN WAS INCREDIBLY NERVOUS but excited that June was coming for dinner that evening. He planned to spend the afternoon shopping for ingredients and then start cooking.

Angelo had been helping him out with the recipes all week. "Love is in the air!" he sang out loud, much to John's embarrassment and the customers' amusement. "You make me feel like a young man again, Johnny boy," he sang. "What a world!"

All of a sudden Theresa called out,

"Quiet, Angelo! Quiet, everybody! There is a special broadcast coming from the palace. Oh my gosh—I hope he's not dead!"

But the news that appeared was the exact opposite. On the small café TV set, the image of Lord Von Dronus appeared and cheerfully announced that thanks to the superlative work of the Royal medical team the King had managed to make a miraculous recovery.

However, the Lord explained, the King's appearance was slightly altered and he assured everyone they needn't be alarmed. Due to the virus that had so aggressively attacked his body, particularly his head, the King had had reconstructive surgery on his face and legs.

Much to John's amazement, the King appeared on screen.

He had quite a long beard, but despite this, John was shocked to see that, whoever his replacement was, he was quite a good likeness.

Everybody in the café cheered "Hooray!" and the sound echoed up and down the street and all across the city.

Amid all the sudden jubilation, John was lost alone in thought.

What does this mean? he wondered. *If I've been replaced by a double, where does that leave the real me?*

When he arrived home later, laden with shopping bags, he noticed that a note had been pushed under his door.

How strange, he thought, and upon reading it, discovered it was an urgently worded message from his old friend the Bootman.

"This is turning out to be the most mysterious day of my life," he said to himself, and then, remembering that his guest was arriving in a few hours, he added, "and, possibly, also the most wonderful one."

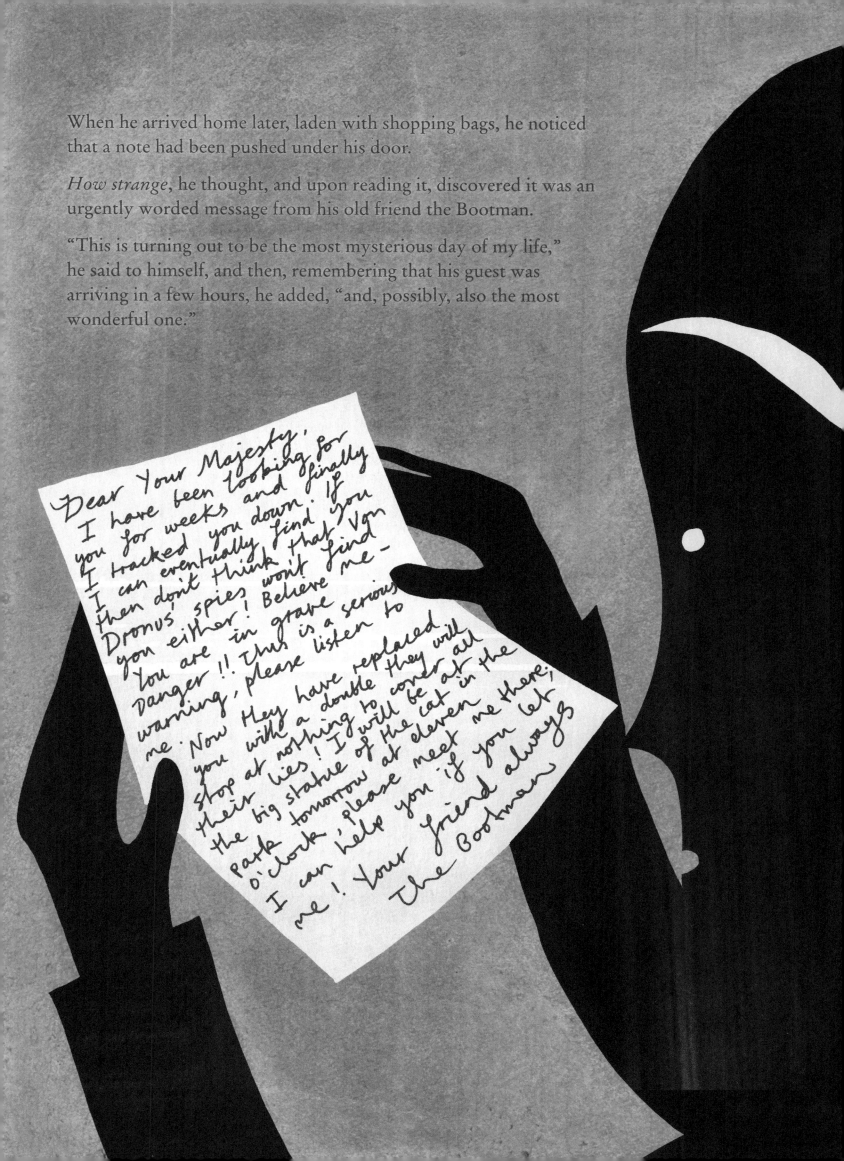

JUNE WAS ALMOST an hour late, and as the minutes slowly ticked by John was beginning to convince himself that she wasn't ever going to turn up, but then suddenly his doorbell rang!

"I'm so sorry I'm late," she said as they climbed the stairs to the attic room, "but so many people were celebrating the King's recovery that all the buses were running slowly."

At the top of the stairs John opened the door to his room.

As she entered she gasped with delight.

"Oh, it's so beautiful!"

Glowing by candlelight, the walls were decorated with thousands of thoughtfully arranged leaves. The table was covered in a cheerful fabric printed with flowers, and from the stove came lovely smells from the food John had prepared.

That evening the conversation flowed easily and naturally. June was funny and quick, but she was also honest and kind, and she was an attentive listener as well as a good talker.

She told him all about her childhood and her school, her parents and her brother and two sisters. She told him how unhappy she was at home, and how she dreamed of getting away one day and forging a new life for herself. She even told him her deepest dreams for herself, and the way she wanted her life to be.

As he listened to June open her heart to him, he felt ashamed that he could never tell her the truth about himself.

"I'm so rude!" she suddenly exclaimed. "I've hardly let you say a word about yourself while I've been talking away."

And almost as if she could tell what he had been thinking, she said, "Some of the folk that come to the van tell you everything that's ever happened to them almost immediately, but then some people never say a single word. Everybody has a story to tell, but it's up to them whether they want to share it."

JOHN TOOK A LONG look at this kind-hearted girl seated on the other side of the table, and realized that of all the people in the world, she was the one he would always want to be true to.

"Believe it or not, I was born in a palace . . ." he started, and then he went on to tell her every detail of his upbringing: his lonely, friendless childhood; Lord Von Dronus' relentless tutorage in how to be a king. He told her all about his friend the Bootman, and the reclusive father he never really knew.

And as he talked and talked, he felt as if a huge burden were floating up from his shoulders. He realized that for the whole of his life he had always held everything that he had ever done or thought deep inside himself; everything he had felt always had to be a secret that he could never really share with anyone.

He told her all about finding the secret trapdoor, and how he had furtively escaped the palace at night and prowled the city streets.

The young woman sat still, slightly wide-eyed at these incredible revelations, but she didn't interrupt; she just nodded as the young man who used to be the King told her his amazing story.

Finally, after telling her all about how he had escaped from the palace, he ended his tale at the point where he honestly felt his old life had ended and his new life had truly begun: "And then I met you."

He stopped talking.

"I always thought that you had an interesting story hidden inside you," she said as she smiled and looked into his eyes.

"And I always liked you anyway, because I just thought you were nice and I didn't care what you were or where you'd come from. I just happened to like you for being you."

And all that night they stayed up and talked and talked and talked about every single thing they had held in their hearts that now they could finally share with somebody else.

As they talked they noticed the room getting slightly lighter as the dull glow of the rising sun began to appear behind the jagged horizon of the rooftops. It was nearly morning.

"Will you ever tell anyone else who you really are, or will you keep it a secret?" June finally asked him.

"I don't know. I only care that you know," John replied.

"What if you marry and have children? Don't they deserve to know who their father really is—who you really are?"

"I don't know," John said. "I suppose I will be the man who loves them, but, yes, I think I would tell them everything. There's so much I haven't even begun to think through."

"What if your children don't want to be like you and don't want to live like you? What if they want to be rich and grow up to inherit the throne?"

"I don't know about that either. I hope they will somehow believe in me. I hope they will realize that I gave it all up for the possibility of somehow meeting someone as wonderful as their mother, the kindest person in the world. And from knowing her and from being brought up and loved by her, how could they fail to then understand completely?"

June blushed and for once didn't know how to reply. After a long pause she said, "I'm starving! I know a café that opens really early. Shall we go and get some breakfast?"

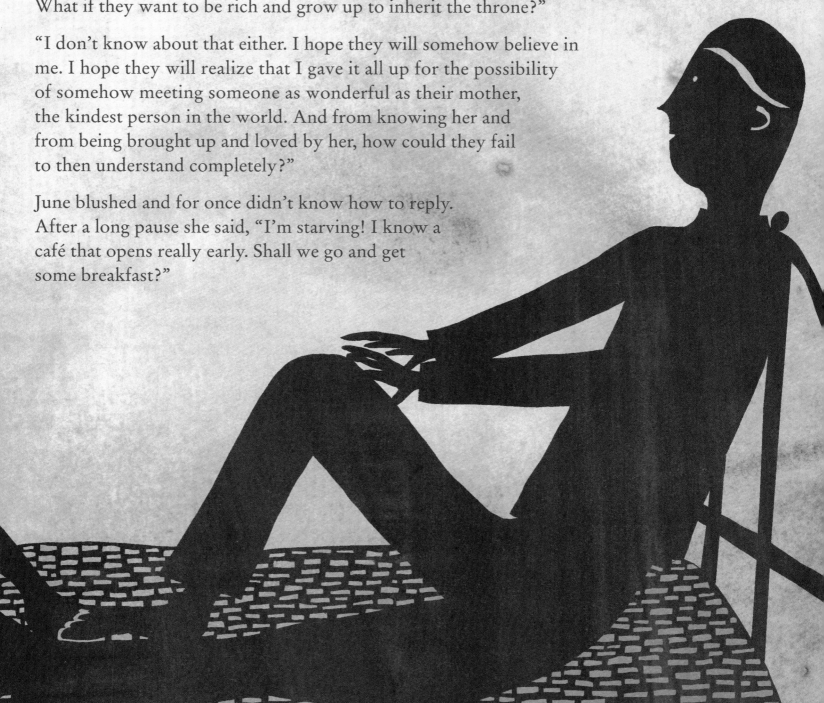

I T WAS A BRIGHT and crisp autumn Sunday morning in the park, and as they walked along its winding paths together, side by side, chatting merrily to each other, they grew closer and closer until John realized that their shoulders were touching. Then he felt a small hand slip into his hand and it stayed there as they strolled along.

Walking down one particular avenue of trees, John looked up and saw the same brightly colored exotic birds were still up there in the branches high above them.

"I saw those birds on the very first morning I left the palace; they seem so different from all the sparrows and pigeons you see everywhere else in the park. It's like they've come from another country altogether—such a mystery," he said.

"Yes, they are quite famous, but only in this particular park," June explained. "But it's not a complete mystery! Years ago it became fashionable among the rich people who lived in the grand houses that surrounded the park to keep rare exotic birds as pets. But occasionally a few of those unlucky creatures escaped from their prison cages and flew across the road to the safety of the trees in the park. People thought these pampered birds from warmer climates than ours couldn't survive out in the wild, away from the heated houses, alone and having to fend for themselves, but against all odds, they did. They met fellow escapees and built nests together, and they thrived and multiplied. To everyone's surprise they managed to forge new lives for themselves in a completely new world."

The young man who used to be King gazed up as he saw these beautiful birds in a new light.

"That sounds not unlike my own story," he said as he turned to face June. "I wonder if mine will have such a happy ending."

June took his hand and held it tightly in hers.

"I can't see how it can be anything but happy if I have anything to do with it," she said, laughing.

And as she put her other arm around his shoulder, she said softly in his ear, "Last night was the loveliest night I have ever dreamed of. All of my life I've been waiting for you to appear, and now you're finally here." She leaned forward and touched his lips with hers.

"You'd better get going to meet your friend," she whispered to him, and quickly kissed him again one last time.

JOHN MADE HIS WAY to the meeting place the Bootman had suggested in his letter. The park was filling up with all types of people: families taking a Sunday stroll, mothers pushing babies in their strollers, people cheerfully walking their dogs.

But of all the hundreds of people there that morning, none felt so alive. For this morning, for this young man, life was not just beautiful, it was perfect.

The events of the past evening, night, and morning had filled his heart with such completeness that he almost felt as if he couldn't endure any further increase in his happiness.

In the distance, he could see the Giant Cat statue, and as he got nearer he could see the Bootman standing by the side of its large pedestal.

John waved cheerfully, but as he got nearer he could see anguish on his friend's face.

"Run! Run away now! Get away!" he cried out to the young King.

Suddenly he felt two pairs of strong hands grasp him firmly by his arms. Stepping out from behind the monument was none other than Lord Von Dronus. He was holding tightly on to the Bootman with one hand, and had thrust a gun into his back with the other.

The Bootman dejectedly mouthed the words *I'm so sorry* before he was silenced by the Lord.

"Congratulations, Your Majesty. I'm glad to see you looking so well," said Von Dronus, his voice laced with sarcasm. "You will be glad to hear that I'm not about to return you to the palace. I'm afraid it's a little late for that."

The last words that John, the young man who had never wanted to be King, heard were full of threat and menace.

"You managed to escape once. Well, now I'm going to help you disappear again—but this time it will be permanent."

And then John felt a crushing blow on the back of his head. Fireworks seemed to sparkle inside his brain for a moment, and then everything went black.

OH, MY DEAR READERS, just as life can be beautiful and generous, it can be cruel.

Sometimes, just when we think all is well and everything seems to be working out just right, fate steps in and sends all our plans and dreams flying up into the air!

After all of the hardships and loneliness this poor young man had to endure, it finally seemed as if love and happiness were around the corner. What now awaits our young friend? What sinister plan does Lord Von Dronus have in store for him? Will he ever get the chance to live his life, not as a king, but as someone free to follow a destiny of his own choosing? I hope it all works out for him, some way, somehow. But I don't have a good feeling about it.

"What a world!"